Rettie and the Ragamuffin Parade

A Thanksgiving Story

Written by Trinka Hakes Noble & Illustrated by David C. Gardner

For Ruby and Ivy
With love,

THN

For my sisters Lilly, Sheree, and Gigi
with all my love.

DCG

Photo Credit, page 32: Bain News Service, Publisher. Scramble for pennies -
Thanksgiving., ca. 1910. [between and Ca. 1915] Photograph.
Retrieved from the Library of Congress, https://www.loc.gov/item/ggb2004010007/.
(Accessed March 27, 2017.)

Sleeping Bear Press®
2395 South Huron Parkway, Suite 200
Ann Arbor, MI 48104
www.sleepingbearpress.com

Printed and bound in the United States.

10 9 8 7 6 5 4 3 2 1

Library of Congress Cataloging-in-Publication Data

Names: Noble, Trinka Hakes, author. | Gardner, David (David Colby),
1959- illustrator.
Title: Rettie and the Ragamuffin Parade : a Thanksgiving story /
written by Trinka Hakes Noble ; illustrated by David C. Gardner.
Description: Ann Arbor, MI : Sleeping Bear Press, [2017] | Summary:
During the 1918 influenza outbreak, nine-year-old Rettie seeks ways to
make Thanksgiving special for her siblings and ailing mother.
Identifiers: LCCN 2017002860 | ISBN 9781585369607 (hard cover)
Subjects: | CYAC: Poverty—Fiction. | Family life—New York (State)—New
York—Fiction. | Thanksgiving Day—Fiction. | Influenza Epidemic,
1918-1919—Fiction. | New York (N.Y.)—History—20th century—Fiction.
Classification: LCC PZ7.N6715 Ret 2017 | DDC [E]—dc23
LC record available at https://lccn.loc.gov/2017002860

*A*ll the tenement children on New York's Lower East Side couldn't wait for the Ragamuffin Parade on Thanksgiving morning. But no one was more excited than a young girl named Loretta Stanowski, whom everyone called Rettie.

All you had to do was dress up like a beggar in old ragged clothes and parade down Broadway. For Rettie, dressing up was easy. She already had holes in her shoes and worn, patched clothes.

Then fancy uptown people would line the streets and call, "Here come the little ragamuffins!" If you held out your hand and asked, "Have ya anythin' for Thanksgiving?" they'd give you a penny.

But the best part of the Ragamuffin Parade happened on busy street corners. Handfuls of pennies were tossed in the air, then all the ragamuffin children would scramble for them. It was called a penny scramble, and sometimes it got rough.

Amelia and little Katalina looked worried. "Rettie, this Thanksgiving, are you going to scramble?" they asked their older sister. This year Rettie was determined to join in. She wanted to buy something special for their Thanksgiving dinner.

"Don't worry," Rettie said as she rocked baby Sebastian. "I'm going to scramble hard and bring home lots of pennies for us."

But that November, in 1918, a great war raged in Europe. Many American men had gone to fight. In America, another war was sweeping across the land, one with an invisible enemy ... influenza.

Quarantine signs had been posted, large gatherings banned, and schools closed. Rettie worried. What if they cancelled the Ragamuffin Parade? She needed those pennies!

Rettie's mama had been sick for a month, weakened by consumption. So Rettie did all the cleaning, washing, shopping, and cooking. She also washed rags for the ragpicker for two pennies a bundle.

After all, she was nine, the oldest. Who else would take care of the family while Papa was a soldier, so far away in Europe? Besides, Mama would get better soon, wouldn't she? But there was no time for worry.

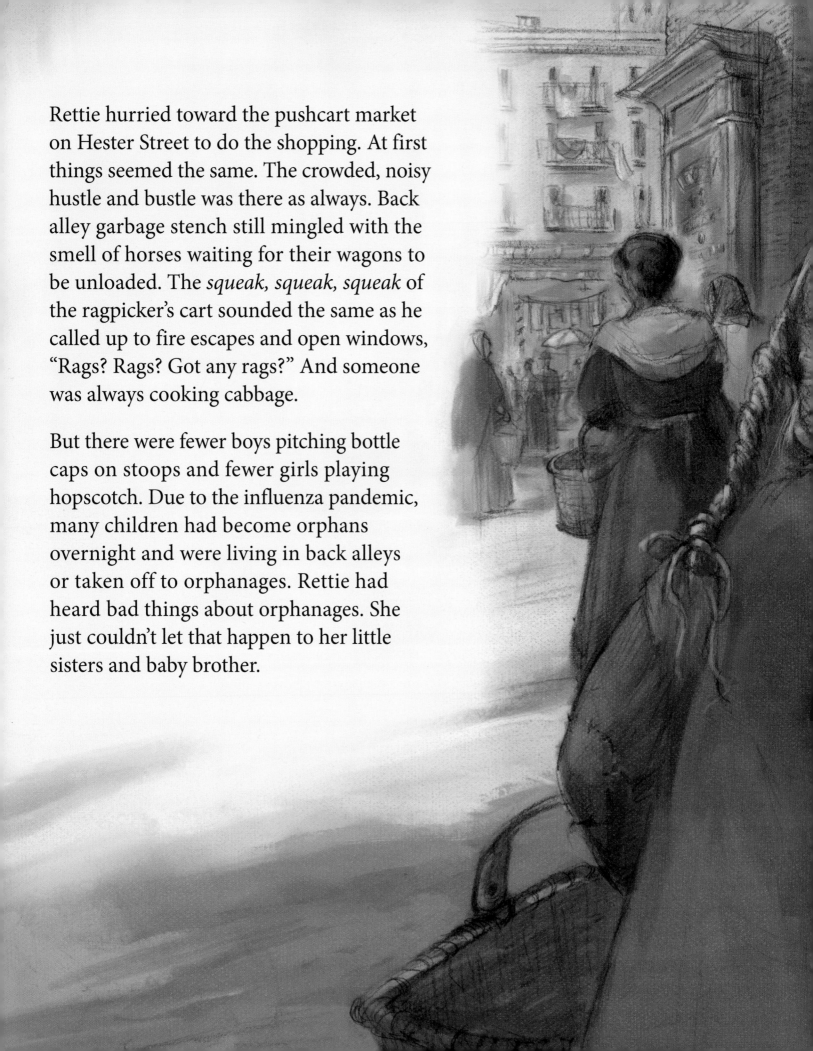

Rettie hurried toward the pushcart market on Hester Street to do the shopping. At first things seemed the same. The crowded, noisy hustle and bustle was there as always. Back alley garbage stench still mingled with the smell of horses waiting for their wagons to be unloaded. The *squeak, squeak, squeak* of the ragpicker's cart sounded the same as he called up to fire escapes and open windows, "Rags? Rags? Got any rags?" And someone was always cooking cabbage.

But there were fewer boys pitching bottle caps on stoops and fewer girls playing hopscotch. Due to the influenza pandemic, many children had become orphans overnight and were living in back alleys or taken off to orphanages. Rettie had heard bad things about orphanages. She just couldn't let that happen to her little sisters and baby brother.

Over on Broadway, the uptown trolley still rattled and clanged, but fewer people rushed to board, and some of them wore masks. And on Hester Street, there were fewer pushcart merchants.

"What, no pickled herring today?" complained Mrs. Goldstein. "How can I feed my family?"

"Schmidt's whole family is quarantined," Mrs. Petrov said with a shrug. "And no beets! I ask you, how can I make my borscht without beets?"

But Zimmermann's bread cart was still there. Rettie
selected two hard, stale loaves. "That'll be six cents,"
said Mr. Zimmermann.

"But my little sisters will break their teeth on these.
I'll give you two cents each."

Then she hurried to Clancy's for one small cabbage and
three mealy potatoes, which she got for a penny each.
Then O'Leary's for two ladles of milk for baby Sebastian.

Rettie had spent all her pennies, but she lingered at Rossetti's fruit cart and secretly ran her hand over the smooth, cool orange pumpkins. Then she breathed in the sweet ripe smell of apples, wishing she could buy them.

Mrs. Goldstein haggled. "Rossetti, these apples fresh?"

"Just shipped down the Hudson River from upstate this morning."

Just then Rossetti spied Rettie. "Shoo, girl! Only paying customers!" he exclaimed, flapping his long apron at her.

When Rettie got home, a health service nurse was posting a quarantine sign on Mrs. Klumpenthal's door.

"But, Nurse Pauline," Mrs. Klumpenthal pleaded. "I manage this building. I must clean the stairs and stoop and empty the ash barrel or the health department will fine me!"

Nurse Pauline was tall, wearing a uniform—a starched white collar, apron, and cap. Rettie had never seen anyone so tidy. She carried a black bag and spoke with authority.

"Ma'am, we must contain the spread of this deadly influenza. No one can leave your apartment."

Quickly Rettie did addition in her head then made an offer. "I'll clean the stairways on all four floors each day, and the stoop for twenty-five cents a week." With Nurse Pauline standing right there, Mrs. Klumpenthal couldn't say no.

Nurse Pauline turned to Rettie, felt her forehead, checked for swollen glands, and said, "Stick out your tongue, child. Good. No influenza. Which is your apartment? I'm checking everyone in the building."

When Nurse Pauline entered the tiny two-room apartment, she saw neatly folded piles of clean rags and more clean rags drying on the fire escape. "Does your mama wash rags?" she asked.

"No, ma'am. I do. Mama's been sick and Papa's away at the war."

Nurse Pauline saw how clean everything was, and how well cared for the younger children were. "You've been doing all this, child? If your mother doesn't get better, and with your father away, do you know what that means?"

Rettie lowered her head and almost cried. "Yes, ma'am." She sighed. "An orphanage."

"Well, let's see what I can do." Nurse Pauline examined Mama. "Good. No influenza." She gave Mama some medicine, then instructed Rettie on the dosage.

"Now, let me inspect your hands," she said briskly. Rettie's hands were spotlessly clean because they were always in soapy water.

"Now keep these little ones inside, but let in fresh air and sunshine each day," she ordered. "Keep everyone's hands clean and, most important, let your mother rest."

Then Nurse Pauline gently touched Rettie's shoulder and spoke softly. "Child, if you follow these instructions, you'd make a fine nurse someday."

So Rettie made a little pretend school under the table. There she taught Amelia and Katalina their numbers and letters while baby Sebastian napped in her lap. She told stories, hummed songs, and played little games, keeping everyone quiet so Mama could rest.

At four o'clock each morning while everyone was asleep, Rettie washed the stairs and railings, swept the halls, and scrubbed the stoop.

The only thing that kept her going was the hope that the Ragamuffin Parade wouldn't be cancelled.

Slowly, with Nurse Pauline's medicine, Mama improved, until one day Rettie helped her walk slowly to the window for fresh air.

On that special day, November 11, 1918, as Mama sat by the open window, they heard newsboys all over the Lower East Side shouting, "Extra! Extra! The War is over!" Then church bells started ringing all over New York.

And for the first time in weeks Mama smiled as Rettie, Amelia, and Katalina danced around baby Sebastian.

Papa would be coming home!

Over the next few weeks, a frigid wind blew through New York and slowed the influenza. World War I was over, and with the return of cold weather, the great influenza pandemic diminished.

America had much to be thankful for this Thanksgiving. So President Woodrow Wilson declared that the 28th of November would be Thanksgiving Day for all Americans to celebrate as one.

But no one was more thankful than Rettie. On Thanksgiving morning she dressed in her everyday patched clothes and worn shoes and proudly marched in the Ragamuffin Parade with her face beaming.

Many people gave her pennies. And, on the corner of Broadway and Broome Street, she bravely entered the penny scramble and added a fistful of pennies to her pockets.

Then she ran to Hester Street with her pockets jingling. Maybe she could catch Mr. Rossetti.

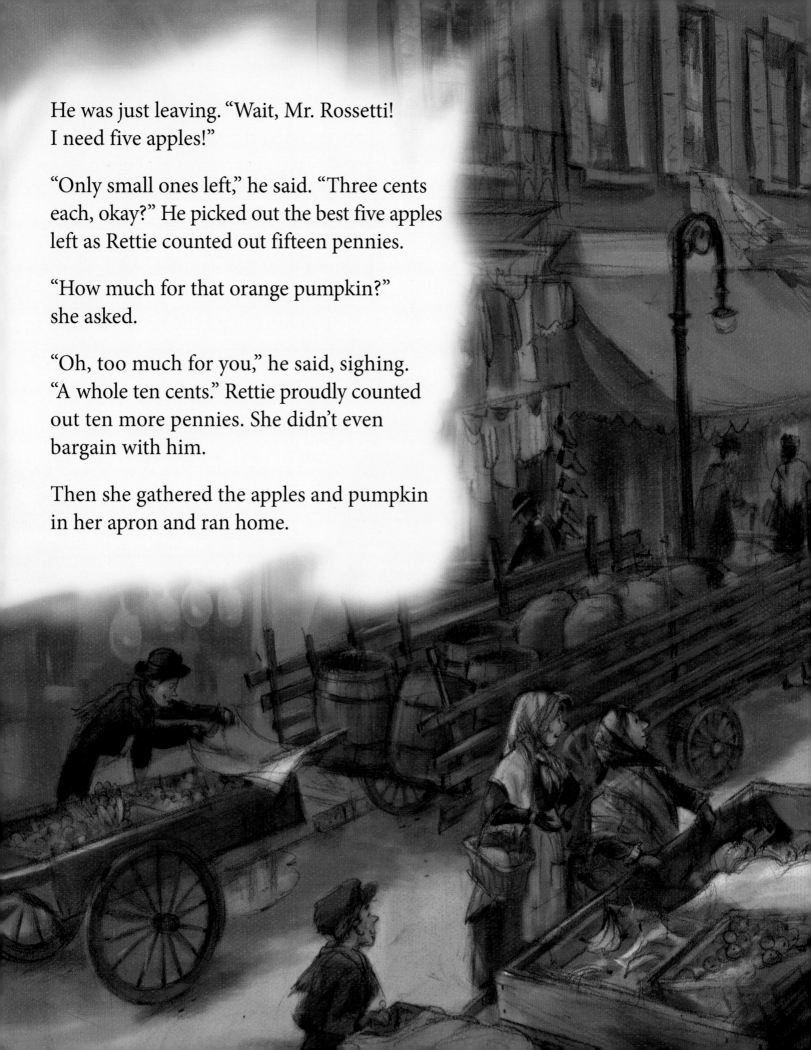

He was just leaving. "Wait, Mr. Rossetti! I need five apples!"

"Only small ones left," he said. "Three cents each, okay?" He picked out the best five apples left as Rettie counted out fifteen pennies.

"How much for that orange pumpkin?" she asked.

"Oh, too much for you," he said, sighing. "A whole ten cents." Rettie proudly counted out ten more pennies. She didn't even bargain with him.

Then she gathered the apples and pumpkin in her apron and ran home.

On that Thanksgiving Day, in 1918, there were many grand dinners and celebrations across America, but none was better than the one set in a small two-room tenement on the Lower East Side. By each bowl of stewed cabbage sat a shiny red apple. And in the center of the table, like the guest of honor, was a small orange pumpkin.

And at that moment, there was no world war, no filth and sickness, no hunger and hardship. Only a young girl's heart filled with the hope of Thanksgiving.

A Thanksgiving scramble for pennies from around 1910.

Author's Note

The Ragamuffin Parade was introduced to New York City in 1870, brought by the many European immigrants who had settled there. Because they wanted to fit in with American holidays, they paired the Ragamuffin Parade with Thanksgiving. On Thanksgiving morning, New York City children would dress up like beggars and parade through the streets with their hands out asking, "Have you anything for Thanksgiving?" People called them ragamuffins and would give them a penny or fruit. The immigrant children who lived in the tenements loved the Ragamuffin Parade because they could fill a pocket with pennies.

But as years went by, Halloween became more popular in America. Children dressed up in costumes, marched in Halloween parades, and went trick-or-treating for candy. The Ragamuffin Parade fell out of favor.

Many immigrant children grew up to be employed by Macy's department store in Midtown Manhattan. They remembered the Ragamuffin Parade fondly.

Some historians believe that these employees asked Mr. Macy if he would sponsor a parade for the children of New York City on Thanksgiving morning. And so, in 1924, the first Macy's Thanksgiving Day Parade took place. It was so successful that it became an annual event, which Americans enjoy to this day.

In 1918 the great influenza pandemic swept across America and around the world. This deadly strain of flu killed an estimated fifty million people worldwide. In comparison, sixteen million died in World War I.

When I was in grade school, an influenza epidemic called the Asian flu swept across America. Many children became sick, including me. That fall I missed four weeks of school, and I also missed Halloween! So my parents bought me a chocolate candy bar and placed it next to my bed to look at until I got better.

I placed this story during America's 1918 great influenza pandemic, on New York's Lower East Side, thinking about how the tenement children would miss the Ragamuffin Parade, just as I missed Halloween.

Copyright © 1999 by Nord-Süd Verlag AG, Gossau Zürich, Switzerland
First published in Switzerland under the title *Kleiner Bär, ich wünsch dir was*
English translation copyright © 1999 by North-South Books Inc.

First published in the United States, Great Britain, Canada,
Australia, and New Zealand in 1999 by North-South Books,
an imprint of Nord-Süd Verlag AG, Gossau Zürich, Switzerland.

Distributed in the United States by North-South Books Inc., New York.

Library of Congress Cataloging-in-Publication Data is available.
A CIP catalogue record for this book is available from The British Library.
ISBN 0-7358-1243-8 (trade binding)
1 3 5 7 9 TB 10 8 6 4 2
ISBN 0-7358-1244-6 (library binding)
1 3 5 7 9 LB 10 8 6 4 2
Printed in Belgium

For more information about our books, and the authors and artists
who create them, visit our web site: http://www.northsouth.com

Marcus Pfister
Make a Wish, Honey Bear!

Translated by Sibylle Kazeroid

North-South Books
New York · London

Honey Bear sat on a rock by the river and stared into the water.

It was his birthday. But Honey Bear was feeling sad.

Only his mother had wished him a happy birthday that morning.

Everyone else had disappeared without a trace.

Had they forgotten?

Suddenly he heard his mother call, "Come here, little birthday bear!"

He headed towards her, then stopped in his tracks.

"Surprise!"

There in the clearing stood his father, his grandmother and grandfather, his sister and his brother,
his cousin, and his best friend.

His mother gave him a big hug. Then she brought
out a beautiful birthday cake and everyone sang
"Happy Birthday."

"Blow out the candles, Honey Bear," said Mother. "And don't forget to make a wish!"

"What will you wish for?" asked his little sister.

What *should* I wish for? thought Honey Bear.

"Wish for all the luck in the world," said Mother softly.

"Wish for many good friends," said his brother,
giving Honey Bear a friendly slap on the back.

"Wish for sunshine every day, wherever you go!"
said his cousin.

"Wish for a big salmon the next time we go fishing," said his father, throwing Honey Bear up in the air.

"Wish for lots of time to play. Especially with me," said his sister shyly.

"Wish for a thick coat, so that you won't get hurt when we wrestle!" said his best friend as he snuck up behind him, laughing.

"Wish for a sharp nose so you'll be able to smell delicious things from far away," said his grandmother, and she gave him a big kiss on the cheek.

"Wish for a long, undisturbed winter's sleep,"
said Grandfather, yawning.

Mother carefully set the cake down on a
tree stump.

Honey Bear closed his eyes, took a big breath,
made a wish, and blew out all the candles.

What did Honey Bear wish for?

Did he wish for all the luck in the world?
Did he wish for many good friends?
Did he wish for sunshine wherever he went?
Did he wish for a big salmon?
Did he wish for lots of time to play?
Did he wish for a thick coat?
Did he wish for a sharp nose?
Did he wish for a long winter's sleep?

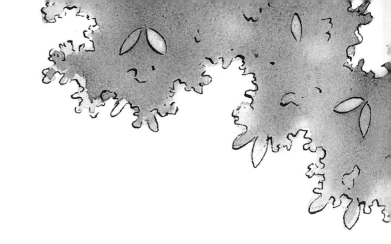

No. Honey Bear wished that *all* his
birthdays could be as happy as this one!